Which One Would You Choose?

by Edith Kunhardt

Greenwillow Books New York

Magic Markers and a black pen were used
for the full-color art.
The text type is Egyptian 505 Roman.

Printed in Hong Kong by South China Printing Co.
First Edition
10 9 8 7 6 5 4 3 2 1

Library of Congress Cataloging-in-Publication Data

Kunhardt, Edith.
Which one would you choose? / by Edith Kunhardt.
p.   cm.
Summary: The reader joins characters Will and Maggie
in choosing articles of clothing, picking out something for
breakfast, and making other decisions as the day proceeds.
ISBN 0-688-07907-5.   ISBN 0-688-07908-3 (lib. bdg.)
[1. Literary recreations.]   I. Title.
PZ7.K94905Wi 1989
[E]—dc19
87-37200   CIP   AC

TO KRISTINA,

FOR HELPING ME CHOOSE

Wake up, sleepyheads!
Will woke up.
Maggie woke up.
Will chose a blue shirt.
Maggie chose a red shirt.

Which one do you choose?

Will liked peanut butter.
Maggie liked cereal.

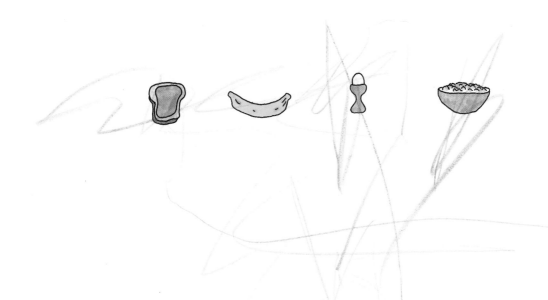

What do you like for breakfast?

Time to go out.

Maggie chose an umbrella.

Will chose a jacket.

Which one do you choose?

The rain stopped.
The sun came out.
After lunch, Will chose
a chocolate ice cream cone.
Maggie chose a vanilla
ice cream cone.

What kind of cone would you choose?

Maggie and Will went
to visit Grandmother.
Maggie carried a daisy.
Will carried a buttercup.

Which flower would you take
to Grandmother's house?

Grandmother's cat had kittens.

Will chose the yellow kitten.

Maggie chose the calico kitten.

Which one would you choose?

Will and Maggie went home.

They took the kittens.

It was time for supper.

Will chose hot chocolate.

Maggie chose orange juice.

The kittens chose milk.

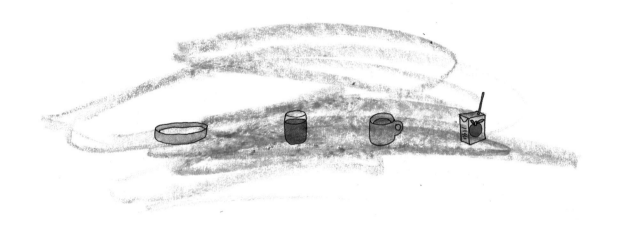

Which one do you choose?

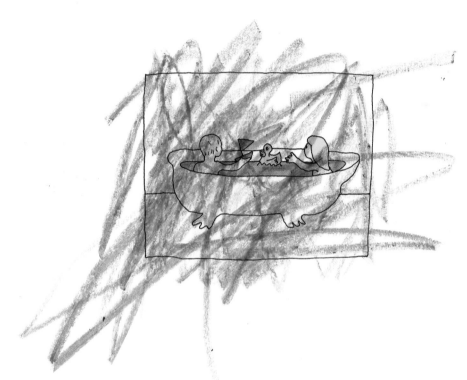

Will and Maggie took a bath.
Will played with a boat.
Maggie played with a duck.

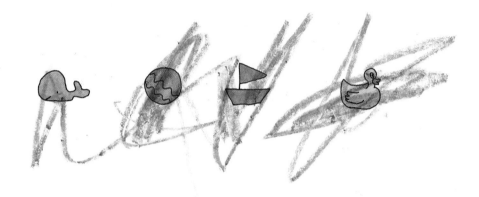

Which toy would you play with?

Will and Maggie brushed their teeth.
Will used his green toothbrush.
Maggie used her red toothbrush.

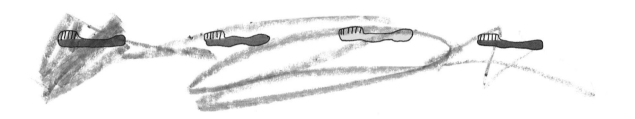

Which toothbrush would you use?

Time for bed!
Will took his new bunny.
Maggie took her old bear.

Which friend would you take to bed?

Good night, Maggie.
Good night, Will.
Sleep well, Maggie.
Sleep well, Will.

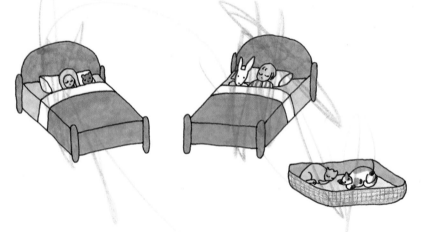

You sleep well, too.
Tomorrow you can choose again.